SCHOOL DAYS

ROHAN KADAM

Title: School Days
Language: English
Character set encoding: UTF-8

First published by

An Imprint of BlueRose Publishers

Head Office: B-6, 2nd Floor,
ABL Workspaces, Block B, Sector 4,
Noida, Uttar Pradesh 201301
M: +91-8882 898 898

DEDICATION

ACKNOWLEDGEMENTS

PREFACE

We all have school memories . They are the part of our growing life which is special to everyone of us. I have fond memories of my school. 'School Days' is a fictional novel of events in school which you make you laugh. All the readers will surely relate the novels with events happened in their innocent and interesting past or present school life. The book has been made interesting because of the hilarious events , fictitious characters and places.

The book is carefully written with the intention of not harming anyone's sentiments. Care has been taken to keep the book free of sexual or racial abuse or caste, greed or gender inequality by following leaders like Martin Luther King, Dr Babasaheb Ambedkar, Chhatrapati Shivaji Maharaj.

The book is self published by me under the ' BlueRose Publishers'. I would like to thank BlueRose for providing me an opportunity to publish this book. It was a dream of my late father, Dr. Ravindra Babaji Kadam to publish a book and I have tried to fulfill his dreams . It would not have been possible without support of my mother Veena Ravindra Kadam, my wife Rutuja Rohan Kadam and my son , Ashay Rohan Kadam. While writing the book , I was helped by my friends Prof. Aniruddha Beladar and school friend Mr Sameer Kamble. I would want my all readers to enjoy their memories of school along with the book .

CONTENTS

HIT AND RUN CASE

'Oops and Batts' was one such weird game or activity which involved hitting others and it surely played by all the children in 1990s. It was a deal of punching on back between two persons. There is an interesting incident related with this 'Oops and Batts'. Gautam and friends decided to just pat on the back with palm. The idea was not to hurt anyone. There are situations where a person look silly, awkward or with less brain cells when the he or she is hit.   It is enjoyment and fun for most children. Comedians and jokers fall to look funny and weird. They are cheered by the audience. The deal game was no different. The rules and the hearts are more transparent which is essence of this game. It is possible only at the tender age that the hit is laughed at but it should not to be used to target anyone. It conversion into revenge seeking device is also harmful.

If you are in the deal, the standing participant should intimate to other opponent by the word "Batts" before sitting and if in sitting position, the same participant should let the opponent know with word of "Oops" before standing .Or else you eligible to get hit as per the rules of the game. Whenever there is change in position, i.e. standing or sitting, you need to let your deal friend know by saying or shouting if you at a distance signaling or gestures were accepted in the deal. Otherwise, you get a pat on your body. When class is going on and teacher's presence is there, signaling was preferred to avoid hit on back. A hit and run incident happened because of 'Oops and Batts' in which Gautam was involved.

Aaron and Gautam had between them 'Oops and Batts 'deal. Talking about Gautam , he was enough tall for a boy of sixth standard class with a well-toned physical body. His hair

es were written all over his face. Aaron was one of the class topper. He was a student who mugged all answers given by teacher. He was more as a bookworm than any other skills and qualitities. All his books were completed before teachers asked for checking. He would be found on first or second bench in the middle row. He was a fair boy with dimpled cheeks and was shorter than Gautam and medium built. He tried to be teacher's pet but the girls, Sakshi and Mary never allowed him to get that position. Sakshi had the best handwriting and was also among the top three rankers of the class, so her notebooks were used by other teachers for making notes if they were not prepared. Mary was the class monitor, sweet girl with brown eyes taller compared other girls in class, slim with black shiny hair and weight proportionate with height. She was liked by most of the staff in the school and also clever enough to get distinction. When she said to class to maintain silence, it was positively approved by the naughtiest boy in class. There was always tough competition between the three for the first rank. They had to really work hard to be ahead of each other. There were talks that the girls worked as a team to keep the male student at the third place.

There was new addition of teachers in the school and the new teacher of science who was tall, well-built man in late twenties. His language made everyone know that he was from south India. He had large eyes and prominent nose. His bearded look differentiated him in the group of others six male teachers. The beard made him look five more years older than his actual age. He had unique way of making students achieve knowledge more than what was given in the textbook. Learning was made effortless by simple words, simpler ideas and the simplest way to make knowledge enter in brain of students. Such was the teaching style of Mr. Rajan Murthy who had also liking for music and singing. He tried to improve his accent by singing different languages especially Hindi. The

ional pronunciation. People get pleasure talking about others when it is none of their business.

Murthy was teaching the chapter for the first time as there was a change in syallbus. The previous portion chapters were in his heart and mind after teaching it for almost eleven years. He did not get time to prepare as he did not have family attention of proper food at proper time. His family was at his native place. He relied on school canteen for lunch and most of times had food in the recess. The canteen was not functioning for some days as the canteen owner's father was ill and had to be admitted in a hospital. Abbas, the lone son had to bear the responsibility to look after his parents and he never ran away from his destined work. The pain of responsibility is not there when one has brothers and sisters. Is a single child overburdened?

It meant getting food from other hotels outside the school or helping himself. He chose the second option. Since the kerosene was over at his place, he had to get it from the market. Because of his inexperience in cooking, he had to redo everything. He managed but it consumed his valuable time of preparation. Mothers play an important role in serving food for the family. How bad cook she would be, she would never let her children go starving at any point in their life.

The time table was set. The lecture was scheduled. Murthy required some extra time for preparation. He could not get more time because a new comer's voice is heard only after senior employees. His joining date was so new that everyone remembered. Murthy had personality by which he could impress others and get benefits. He used to sing in school assembly after the national anthem. Even the principal of the school also liked this talent. On that day, his singing fell short to get time for preparation. Murthy trying to delay the science period by asking lecture after recess, but was without success.

He entered the class with half hunger and a bit of dejection. He decided to take control of the situation and manage it somehow. Why not take students to perform an experiment? Fifteen to twenty minutes would be utilized in taking students to the lab , such thoughts were playing in his mind to engage the students and hide the unpreparedness. He was not sure which experiment, as brain often does not function at times in panic. So an expert companion is of a great help but he had none. He sent Aaron to get the keys of the lab.

The 'Oops and Batts' game between Aaron and Gautam was only a day old. It started in last period the previous day so both the players were dying make the first hit on each other. The first day was unproductive for the two. So the next day, they had made up their minds to have fun by making other look awkward. When Aaron got up , Gautam's eyes became wider knowing that he would get a chance to hit him.

Gautam almost became restless to seize the chance and the distance between them was only of two benches. But he checked the emotions because he did not want to be punished for not paying attention in class. Aaron returned back saying , "The lab assistant is absent and so the set up is not ready", he said with a depressed tone. The whole class including Aaron wanted to perform the experiment which was not decided. Murthy gave such a look to the clock in the class as pleading time to run faster. It was a new clock with picture of a freedom fighter and dark coloured hands showing the exact time .All the classes had such clocks with pictures of freedom fighters reminding of their sacrifice. Murthy was not able to identify the leader as he was only interested in clock showing time 9.30 a.m. The shorter hand calmed his nerves to some extent. His eyes were seeing the longer hand as if telling it to skip normal routine . Today, he wanted the earth to revolve faster . He wished he could have had such powers for a day.

Sadly, he realised that for next thirty minutes ,he had to manage the class being only normal human.

He thought of asking questions and get answers of students but the lesson was not completed enough so his brain started to find other ideas. Trying to get an idea, he took chalk in his hand and wrote the name of subject on the black board along with the date. He talked to himself,"May be today is not my day . My complaint would go to principal and my job will be in danger". Suddenly the importance of job, the worth of money in his life troubled him and was blaming himself for this situation .Till now , he was facing the board, his back was towards the class.The thought of job in danger made him determined to face the class.

He was saved a girl and her question came to his help. Kumud, a below average scoring girl was absent on the day before, asked a question on the demonstration . She always kept her books well covered , properly labelled and importantly completed. Her handwriting was close to typed form but logic in exams would always fall short of the expected. The main only thing lacking was remembering the notes in exams, making more teachers and parents believe in the saying that human brain does not work in love and in exams. She never failed in exams and had to be satisfied with lower second class.

The demonstration was taught was by him from textbook on that day.She asked " Murthy sir, can you explain the leaf demonstration again? I was absent ", with a requesting tone and a usual doubt on the face.Murthy eyes lit up when there was realization that the topic would be enough for the remaining period time. The relief was evident in his voice and his words became better pronounced. Suddenly , there was purpose in his stride and his actions became full hearted.

The leaf experiment was latest addition to the textbook. It was to prove that leaves emit carbon di oxide from the hind side of the leaf. Gautam had studied the experiment. Murthy instructed, " The student, I pick would give explanation of experiment", sending a mild pressure on most of the students. Students standing last in ranking and those failing had more pressure of same sentence of the teacher. Thus, it was the hide and seek time where such pressurized students hide behind tall students in front of them.

Gautam had the habit of reading the textbook knowing about the chapter before the teacher. He was good at English and hence reading once was enough to make sense to him. He read the entire chapter for sake of curiosity .He knew the experiment thoroughly . Murthy was unprepared and was utilization the time . He threw the question saying ," We discussed half of the chapter till the experiment and conclusion. Some students have doubts , wants revision on it". The last sentence was said by him with eyes fixed on Kumud.All the class started finding the page in the text book including the hide and seek players.

Now, to hear the bell for recess was not only in his mind but also in the minds of under pressure students and their senses were working on it. He could have asked the question to Aaron, or Kalpana or Sakshi who battled for the top rank in the class. And he thought if the answer was given early then his unpreparedness would be in front of the class . His non-permanent job will be taken away. The thoughts made him realise that such student should be chosen who would not give answer. Atleast, the first three students should be of non answering category so that period can be dragged. The time was spent by Murthy ,taking the chance to scold the students for not studying seriously and only intending to pass in exams. He said ," Student should study regularly to understand the concepts. Merely passing will not help.Whenever a question is asked , every one must be in position to answer it." By giving his own example, he said," I studied every day . All bright students have the habit of not skipping studies even a single day." All teachers say about everyday studying. Gautam wanted to explain the experiment but thought came to his mind about if teachers are so excellent then why they do not pursue IAS or become CEO or hold position of Director in any multi national company or top business tycoon or the Prime minister or union cabinet or state minister.Before the thoughts could make a meaning, The question was raised ,"What are the findings of the experiment?". This was the second time the question was thrown in front of the class and every one eyes were on Gautam who was known to give answers in such unplanned questioning. He waited for the first four rankers to give the answer but to his surprise none of them knew the answer. "If no student from this class answers then all will have to write the answer thrice as homework for tomorrow". The thoughts of savior came to his mind and he stood in a fraction of second .

Gautam gave the answer above expectations of the teacher. All the topper students felt they missed an important part in their studies because they failed to answer. The answering session was enough to utilise the remaining time of the lecture. The teacher realizing that lecture time nearing to its end, was satisfied that the lecture went without any troubles. He wanted to thank two students , first was Kumud for raising the question but thanking her could mean showing his weakness of that day. So he thaked her only in his mind . The second was Gautam for answering perfectly enough for all students to understand. He was about to thank him   but something was more important happened. It was the much awaited ringing of the recess bell. The bell rang sending vibration in the physique of Murthy. He wanted to dance and shout but all that possible in the class was the involuntary and special happiness on his face.

Gautam did not bother about the not receiving the appreciation. All he wanted was to hit on the back Aaron. No sooner did the bell rang than all students stood up including Aaron. Murthy was the first to leave the class as always which the students liked about him in addition to his teaching.There was no verbal or non verbal signal from Aaron because of urgency to go to washroom. The atmosphere was cold to make students rush to the washroom. Gautam was following Aaron and made sure he was behind just enough not to make his deal friend notice him and lose the chance. To avoid any further delay because of the crowd , Aaron decided to use the staff washroom which was against the rules of the school .But the nature call made him to go against the rules and Gautam became follower in rule breaking.

On the left side of the staff washroom was staff room and on the right side was stairs. Aaron used the stairs and was followed by Gautam .Murthy sir was walking towards the washroom from the staff room and Gautam hit Aaron as he was about to enter the wash room and Gautam shouted in joy "Oops".Aaron received a hit on back and was not happy about it as his face made it evident . As per the deal , he was about to accept it but interrupted by Murthy's presence. He hurriedly came at the spot on hearing the noise. The eyes of the teacher became red with anger on seeing Gautam hit Aaron.

Seeing the worst expressions on his teacher's face and the punishment to follow, Gautam did not know what to do and bell rang to mark the end of recess. It gave him an easy chance to get away at that the critical time. The thoughts flooded in his mind that the worst was yet to come. Sir would complaint to his class teacher. His parents would be called in school and will have to be audience of unpleasant listening where the principal would act like King , Murthy on left would be the commander in chief . Flower teacher, the class teacher be sim-

ial effects , para language at its best to create a larger than life scene. Gautam would be the culptrit or the offender and will have to look down all the time paining his neck.

He was good at answering questions in class and he had proved to that in the class to Murthy sir . His ability and intelligence must be accepted as a compensation for is hitting act, his mind told him .He gave the answer in the just concluded lecture and so he should be spared from the punishment . Never before he such idea struck that his answers in class would be of such use one day.

Luckily the next day was Saturday. He said to himself , "The weekend could save me, Saturday and Sunday were made to save people from mistakes made on Friday".Murthy had the habit of forgetting things especially the homework given on Friday. It got checked on Monday due to monitor's job of reminding . The memory problems gave him hopes of getting out of hit and run case. Gap of three days would be better than two days to forget any incident which was in the mind of teacher, thought Gautam. He decided not to go to school as he wanted to avoid the punishment episode. Avoiding school would require a strong reason and he was searching for it.

He could find any logical reasoning till Sunday afternoon. On the Sunday evening, his is aunt came home, giving him the reason. Sumi Suryavanshi entered by saying,"You and your family will definitely enjoy the Mongolian Rice." The joy of making could be heard in her voice. It said that Chinese food elements are hard to digest, then the Mongolian food would a step further , more likely to cause indigestion . His brain took this logic as reason for not going to school and the story started taking shape. He was enjoying how things were falling so perfectly in place for the so called leave. She left handing the food to Gautam.

His aunt always tried new recipe shown on 'Food Special' channel . She was always eager to cook those dishes which were rarely heard .She was a lady in her late thirties was expert in cooking only those dishes which were aired on the channel. Mostly , it was to show love to her family members including her husband's mother. Only a small amount was taken by the elder woman but happy to see her daughter-in-law interest in cooking. Sumi's cooking when compared with her mother in law , was at the beginner stage.Her husband had to face the task of appreciating all those without knowing the ingredients, tasting and eating enough to keep her heart.

Gautam always took a small amount with doubtful mind. But this time, his mind was asking to go for larger quantity. Vini, his mother was a gracefully aging lady in her late forties . Her manners and her living ways gave message of her education and her approach towards life. She had less wrinkles as compared to other ladies of her age. She knew to handle life which was evident from the energy seen in her.

He did not ask mother to taste or eat it as she was in 'Do Not Disturb' mode watching her favourite serial. Only ads were breaking her link with the actors . She was stuck in the place and the remote was untouched even in the ads. The foreign dish was tastier than the previous experimental food which was other reason for him to eat it completely. After the serial , she rushed to the washroom as the serial was more important than any interruption. Then she asked for some rice to taste. Seeing the empty bowl , she looked at him with stunned face and said with surprise," You never eat aunt's food that much ." she said further , " Sumi seems to made it better and she is improving", being happy for Sumi." You should have kept something for me. I like to taste new dish," she said commandingly .

He had eaten the rice so that it would be easy to prove that it affected him .After half an hour , he decided to suffer from stomach ache. His mom was preparing to make evening dinner.He went to his room and checked his expressions of pain in mirror whether , the expressions looked real and then hold on to one. He decided to bring his acting to help him and 'His Movie' started . The first dialogue was in a low tone , keeping hand on his left side of stomach ," Mummy, my stomach is paining . I am feeling like vomiting ". With concerning tone and taking him closer to her , She asked , "What happened? " With right hand on the stomach , he said showing pain in his voice , "I am not well…. Something wrong with my stomach ." His mom further enquired , " Is it because…of outside food or…. Or Sumi new dish?.... Who told you to have the entire thing".The tension made her to say all about manners . The tone was higher about principles of life.

He had no other option but to blame his aunt and her food.   The excuse that aunt food experiment affected seemed better than any other. Suddenly, she became savior for him in the hit and run case. Previously , he always criticized her for using him and his parents as 'food analyst' and to get feed-back . It shows nothing is permanent , a bad person becomes good as situation changes.

She wasted no time and called Sumi but the line was busy. With dejection and anger, she kept down the phone. After few minutes , Sumi called back and it was received be-fore the first ring ended. At first , Sumi was surprised that none from her family had a stomach upset and was liked so much that she repented for giving away a part of it. She felt more better when aunt on phone said , "I have a special liquid , means a syrup which cures all kinds of stomach ailments." She also specified that solution was prepared on lines and ex-perience of Baba Bhismadev. He personally was on the show ,' Permanent Remedy' to help the society. It was prepared by her to cure everybody. The voice sounded the pride of making so called remedial liquid.

The relief was changed into worry when thought of never used before came to her mind. But it was Sunday late evening and doctors were difficult to find and chemists shops out of their business hours. The 'Day and Night' chemist was further away and his father had gone to their village , so someone was required to fetch the proper medicine. Giving a small dose would not do any harm, she thought. She also decided not to repeat the medicine under any circumstance. The previous stock of medicine was out of their expiry date. With no option left , he would be the first to consume the medicine.

No medicine should be taken without eating some food. So she just decided to make rice water soup so that her son can have it. It is easily digested and also helpful to give much needed energy to sick person. She like any selfless mother was forced to have same dull and tasteless sick people's food as dinner along with Gautam . Ranvir , aunt's husband called asking if he could get proper medicine from the Day and Night Chemist. Maybe , his mind did not approve of the Baba's solution and it was the same reason that he did not come to hand over the liquid . Sumi was confident about the solution and this time he had to listen to her. She brought the liquid to Gautam's house.

Sumi came again with her unused relief giving liquid in night dress just taking a shawl and without properly kept hair. She returned in no time because of house chores. The problem creator and solution finder in the eyes of Vini was Sumi but in real Gautam was fake illness creator.

He had to consume the rice soup if he wanted leave tomor- row , he had a deal with himself. It made him realize that any- thing false requires a price to pay.

Finishing her food early, not taking enough taste , she rushed to his room to find him sleeping. She cared for him and wanted him to take the medicine. There was a sudden realization which made her happy and sad in that same moment. She said to herself, If a person sleeps soundly , it means he has no health problem and if any , it was under control. Knowing he was fine, removed her from all the negative thoughts and she became relieved. The tension and wrinkles of the face reduced. Why was he lying, the question in her mind mixed her happiness with curiosity. And the reason to know the truth removed the positive feeling from her mind. She had caught one thing and it was time for the final arresting and checkmating the culprit. She had to plan for getting the real thing from his mouth. All mothers have special tasks to perform in the upbringing of the children and this was no different.

The next morning , he got up forgetting about the cooked up sickness.He took a look form window to see train passing , people even at early hours trying to keep their commitments. It gave him motivation and mental push to start his day. His eyes went on to the old woman , struggling to climb the railway bridge and was able to climb buy with the help from a passer-by. That time he realized about his planned condition he should be in. He changed his stiff normal walk into slow lethargic one. Pain was brought back on his face to have an effect of a sick person. He enacted the fake illness with the intent of not being caught. He had not told her that he would not go to school as she might sense the fakeness. The thought of doing things at a reduced pace came to his mind so that it would be late for school and even mom herself would not sent him to school. Or he would be slow and act as if his condition can go bad   so that she herself would ask him not attend school for a day. These two options were in his mind leading to a sure avoiding school.

She woke on time to for her breakfast and his tiffin. She prepared one of his favourite dish for breakfast called 'Thali peeth'. This was done on purpose as they were a part of the plan which involved tempting him and getting the secret. She made them in more numbers as she was sure that after truth is out , he would have them more than usual. She could wake him and get the reason but she wanted him to accept his mistake and reveal the truth.

After his slowest bath , he came with same pace to have his breakfast . Since morning he did not make any eye contact with his parent. She was giving out expressions that she knows alteast half of the condition .She offered him rice water soup and said , "This will make to feel better without causing any trouble to your stomach." She ate infront of him his favourite dish without sharing even a small piece . This never happened before and she could see both expressions surprise and the hurt on his face of not having any. She was teasing him with a good amount of quantity of ' Thaali Peeth ' right in front of him. She could see and feel the mouth watering moment he was experiencing . All mothers can see inside out .But he changed his place making excuse that he felt cold under the fan. The first attempt failed.

The next attempt involved bitter medicine. No child likes to consume bitter thing with or without a reason. His mother told him to take medicine and go to school.He replied ," If I go to school and something goes wrong then .My case can worsen," the last sentence was said with bit of burp purposely and hand on lower part of tummy. It was to make illness look real. She answered controlling her emotions and showing extra love, " Beta , the medicine is to give you relief. It is bitter but as you know without pain there is no gain." The bitter word making him angry on himself as why he had plan stomach ache and why Murthy sir had to catch him . He hated the' bs' badly , first was bitter and other was Bhismadev.He had seen such people in cartoons and films and to trust them was out of question.

He decided in his mind that somehow he must avoid consuming the so called medicine. It required to use all his skills or else his mother would know he was not sick.And all these thoughts making him impatient. Trying to sound normal,he said ," You are experimenting on me along with Sumi aunty. The liquid would give relief is unknown , how can you be so sure? What if my stomach blasts? He further said , I slept the whole …… night….. ." And   realized that he said something which he should not have come out of his mouth. She gave a stern look to Gautam and it was enough for him to understand that things are not what they seem . The cat was out of the bag. The experienced mother's second attempt was fruitful.

She said in motherly strong voice, "Get up now , you are already late". This statement was the final in the coffin. He realized that there no point in answering . The things went her way and the sickness vanished without any medicine. But the verbal disclosure of exact cause of falling sick was more significant as it would not only let her know but also solve the false matter . It would help her to stop happening it again . The learning through events of life shapes a person . It takes a responsible person to help moulding the future of younger ones. She wanted to do exactly the same.The habits, the manners and future can thus be said are defined by parents.

She made the surroundings in right tone for the talk. After he had finshed , she touched his left shoulder. Caressing it, asked in loving tone ,"What's the matter? What was the reason of saying false?" She took him closer when the last question was asked.

He answered plainly for the first time with eye contact , " I did not want you to face bad music from the Principal and teachers." Then he told all about the game and rules , the hitting and Murthy sir finding him at the wrong moment . She smiled and her tension eased in her eyes which he could not understand. She said , "When you have done nothing wrong, never be afraid. It was just a game where hitting is taken as fun . It is liking pulling leg of friends where one hits and the other cannot hit back. But there are better ways of having fun with friends."As it is not wrong what you have done, I fully support you and I will be on your side.His movements became normal again. She got the specially made ' Thalipeeth ' for him and even gave him extra as all mothers having calculating scale made of love. Love of mother is more intense than any other force or divine power.

Now , the strengthening factor was mom , the support was there after the secret of illness was out. Why he delayed hiding the reality from his mom? His mind questioned him. Then there would have been no reason to perform the drama . Time would   not have been wasted in playing a sick person. Bringing in Sumi auntie and her love of cooking food in the story for no fault of hers. The cause of the unwanted was love for his parents , he hated the thought of them get insulted .Again , there was a debate in his mind. But now, the solution was his mom.

He went to school with the positivity in his mind all the way but seeing the gate , changed him . Before stepping into the gate of school, the idea of avoiding school by going some-where else seemed logical to his mind.   It will add to list of false , he calculated. To cover or hide a lie will enlarge it. Making himself mentally better, he decided to say sorry about the incident .On unlucky days a person is caught or abused without any faults of theirs. And on lucky days, a person is spared and unpunished even he or she is involved in the wrong act. He wished today was one of the lucky days and the hitting was part of the play, he pleaded to himself.

Gautam was late to school than any other day but he still he tried to end the matter by finding Murthy sir before the lectures. On Mondays, science lecture was no there in his class . So the hit and run case will take more time to get solved ,thought Gautam. The first lecture was of History teacher,

ents as it used to be full of hilarious examples and explanation. That day, she was unwell and all the students still expected the usual creativity and enthusiasm . Their dejection was clearly seen on the faces even when they tried to hide it. For Gautam , the day was bad till now .

He was tired and bored of thinking what would happen when he apologizes . He could not concentrate on his studies . He was not knowing how to approach the teacher . He did not want others to know so he avoided taking permission from other teachers in his class and meet Murthy sir. He also suspected that all teachers are aware about the hitting case but behaving normal. The negative thoughts that Murthy would punish him after personal discussion or ask him call his mother as a punishment were not leaving him.

Teachers can call students in whenever they are free or also in lectures . Murthy sir should have that done in first lecture so that the tension in his mind would not be kept building for so long time. The wait time ended the in the fourth lecture which was before the break . A monitor from other class came to him before the next teacher. He said in commanding tone, " Murthy sir has called you in staff room immediately after the class." The messenger was taller than boys of his age and sturdy to make Gautam think of the future had outcome of meeting could be harsh. The day was taxing as in the first two lectures they had to do writing work .

He went to meet Murthy sir as he could take the notes later from other students. He got the permission to meet in the lecture hours which was first good thing to happen . It was relief from boring and head breaking day.

The other better feeling he got was that he was not called during the recess time by Murthy sir. He could atleast enjoy his food in sufficient time. This was second better act. The next thing was the lift offered by the Principal till the first floor.The reason for the special treatment was the messenger boy who was his favourite student.All the three suggesting that the rest of the day would end in his favour and more importantly Murthy sir decision.

He had to go alone to the staff room as the principal had to discuss with the prefect. There would be support for Murthy in form of other teachers, such thoughts gathered in his mind. The bombardment would be from all sides , he made up his mind to be tougher to face the awaited meeting. He did student monitoring of teacher 's voice to find which teachers were in and the number before entering the judgement room. The naughtier the student is the more accurate the recognition of the teacher's voices. He could not do voice recognition as there was silence . The teachers were busy in their lectures which was the fourth pleasant event making him believe that he could expect the good day ahead.

There was a big round table with chairs arranged in circular manner. Murthy was alone in the room , sitting on his usual place which was the chair opposite to the door. He was reading today's editorial and always wanted to enjoy each and every word without any interruptions. He did not care about the happening around him and so his behaviour could be termed as lost . He was in relaxed position making maximum use of the chair.

He asked for permission , " May I come in ", in his lowest tone just enough to let the teacher aware of his presence. Sir had reached the second last word of editorial. Gautam searching for the eyes of Murthy to understand the mood . Murthy adjusted himself in an erect posture before he said come in to the student still reading the editorial. The teacher permitted the him in the staff room with a normal tone calmed his nerves. He stopped his paper work and said plainly, "The experiment we discussed in the last lecture is proven to be from syllabus. Did you knew about it". He could not believe what he was hearing . Smile broke on Gautam's face and got noticed by Murthy. Then he asked Gautam , " Did you know about it already? You said in the class that the answer could be interpreted in another way also." Gautam kept his emotions in check and answered , "I heard it from my farmer uncle . The textbook did not support the view so it created doubts in my mind. " Both agreed that the correction needs to be done in education field at the earliest and not at the will of the government or any political party.

The bell rang to signal the end of conversation. Gautam was relieved that the 'Oops and batts ' event also ended with the bell. The thought about the reason for the teacher's behaviour came to his mind but the hunger thoughts are more stronger and same was with him.

When the hunger is high the ordinary food becomes extra ordinary delicious. The taste of every bit was delicious as the incident was solved . Undue stress affects the taste more than cooking or the ingredients . The next four lectures were enjoyed by him which all were his favourite subjects . He answered most of questions in History and Maths lectures..The drawing lecture was always enjoyed by all students even by those who were bad in drawing. He even found writing Geography and notes more meaningful than usual. His face and the time was shining but Murthy sir came as a shadow ten minutes before the end of the last lecture. The effect was like an eclipse same as on the moon turning his face into a dull coloured one. Was there a twist in tale? All stories end in happy note! Why not his? Has sir remembered punishment? Will the incident have a sad end"? Did Aaron complained to Murthy sir? All these questions came to his mind all together but with no answers. Murthy sir interrupted the Geography class after making an excuse to Shelly miss. He came at the centre of the table and signaled the students to sit who had got up to say 'Good afternoon'. He found Gautam on the second bench in the third row who was standing thinking over what was happening in his teacher's head. He knew that he had to wait after the class before Murthy sir said. When sir was saying same thing , he was so lost in his imaginary sad end that he could not hear. Murthy sir left the class and took with him the boy's happy face. His actions became slower and he could hardly pay attention to Shelly miss. His mind was occupied with thoughts of Murthy sir that he should have finished the hitting case in the first instance. All teachers insist that work should not be kept pending for next time. Now, that the event was forgotten in lecture before recess , why it has come up . If the teacher has recollected even then the outcome should not be changed like during examination once the answer paper is given then students are not allowed to change if any student recollects the answer. His mind gave an explanation to support his view.

The afternoon bell did not disappoint the students as everyday with the sweet sound marking the end of that day . The same bell with same tune is hated at the start of the day. For Gautam , there no differentiation today in both the ringing sounds. Sameer ,his best school friend said that he would not accompany while returning home on that day. No student wanted to have any interference involving Murthy sir. He had to meet Murthy sir alone .

He wanted the ghosts of the hitting case to be put to rest permanently. Now, he realized that sooner he meets the teacher the earlier he could be relieved. His slower movements changed to a faster mode . He had done everything possible within his limits to avoid the hit and run matter. He fell sick , blamed the innocent aunt and fate also favoured him in the first 'One On One'. He went to staff room with purpose and found Murthy sir waiting on the same chair. There was no teacher except him but he had company of the house keeping employees. The nervousness or effect of people present there, was nothing as he was ready with the phrase'I am   sorry' which has more impact in any situation.

He stood at the centre of the staff room door to ask to enter . He looked relaxed as compared in the previous fourth lecture meet. But instead of permitting him, stood up came close to Gautam , seeing in his eyes , Murthy said, "Come let's go on the ground." He replied tensely , "Sir , I want to say… sorry …..about….". He was interrupted by the teacher, " You are an excellent student with commendable knowledge. I spoke to Aaron about the incident that there was a deal between you two about hitting and having fun."

"When someone is hit, he or she is in awkward position as cannot hit back because of the hitting deal game. There is also a competition who hits the more number of times and enjoys the undue advantage. I would not support such a thing. You can have in many other ways. Sports is a good way to win by competing, sharping skills and defeating the opponents. Your friends become your opponents just for the game. There is no physical hitting when played by following rules. It is best option of having fun, building a good physique and developing skills, respect and sportsmanship." This all was said passionately by Murthy while they were coming downstairs to reach the playground. He was following sir who had maintained eye contact throughout the conversation.

Murthy sir took a football in his hand and said intently, " I can also join you every Saturday to play football with your class after permission from the principal. Friendship should be enjoyed without pain and belittling others ."

The hit and run case was closed and forgotten after he promised the teacher to avoid giving pains to his friends. He happily went home and shared the entire day events with his mom.

NAME SAME

The team of Shri Shahu Maharaja English High school was never able to get to winning ways because of the 'Cheap selector' Vinod, as Gautam used to call him. The head boy , Vinod was the captain and also the Chief Selector of the Cricket team in the school. He was the tallest boy in his class , strongly built having a lot of attitude. The selection was done only favouring his friends by Vinod. The players were selected were close to Vinod and company.The team practiced hard enough but never produced win as a result. The way the bat was held was telling the everyone that those hands never ever had played any sport. Gautam's raising voice against Vinod helped Pranay get a place in the side . He had to complain straight to the Principal . Thus revenge relation started between him and Vinod. The same name advantage was taken by Gautam in one such incident to come out of the revenge.

Vinayak Sharma, the Physical Education teacher was wearing dark black coloured T- shirt on which 'Physical Training teacher' was written in bold orange colored with a visibly larger font. He was saying to the boys in a high tone, " I have given the responsibility of selecting and training to the captain of the school cricket team".

Before the complaint of Gautam, the head boy had final say in cricket selection or any sport major decisions. The Physical Education teacher had made himself free from all kind of selection .He was an expert in Hindi who disliked opportunity of teaching Physical Education. Saying no to management would mean losing his bread and butter.The expenses of the school were in control mode only because not having a separate teacher. Gautam's friend, Pranay had great affinity

cricketing talent made the success graph move upwards. Vinod had to lose captaincy to Pranay.

Only Gautam knew Pranay weakness as a batsman, like all close friends know of each other. He was blackmailed that the secret can go to Vinod. All the wishes of Gautam were satisfied enough so that the secret never reached Vinod's waiting ears. Pranay was also monitor of the class, so his occasional chatting in absence of the teacher went unpunished, if the homework was pending by mistake, Gautam's books did not reach teacher's desk thanks to the Pranay. Gautam wanted to have ice cream after school. So he said pointing towards the recently opened ice-cream parlour and in an animated tone said ," We will have ice-cream of chocolate flavor after school." Pranay replied disapprovingly," I cannot have it or else tomorrow's match will be over for me.I am having cold , it may increase. Vinod will get the chance to lead against St Xavier's , a weaker side and he will overjoyed to prove his cricket skills." Gautam in disrespecting tone said further, " Vinod does not deserve to play in our school team but we should not make him lucky."They decided that ice cream party will be after the match is won under able leadership . The decision showed that Gautam wanted his friend to excel in life and his love for him.

The principal was convinced easily after seeing the results.New players deserved place in the eleven. The results could be seen into positive zone and his friend's popularity grew head and shoulders above the head boy.

Vinod wanted to see Gautam in a bad situation and so searching for something against him. He wanted to seek revenge about his losing captaincy and hold over the team affairs. The day came with that chance where he was acting as a victim of some 'gruesome crime' as the term used by him. He complained to teacher Ms Sandra Flowers, the class teacher of sixth class was also heading the disciplinary committee. A lady in her early twenties with brown eyes and smile that could melt toughest of hearts. She also had the ability to change herself in a strict teacher when students tried to take undue advantage. She asked him what happened , he replied "Some boys from her class purposely splashed water on him in the recess. Their leader is Gautam who is a monster . He insulted me infront of everyone . He always torments me in some way or other". He also used his tears to support himself.

Gautam along with his friends was playing and due rainy season, water had accumulated in the ground area. While running behind his friends , he accidently splashed water on someone. After stopping , he realized it was Vinod. He apologized to Vinod. Due to his the narrow mindedness, Vinod said angrily, " I will give answer of your action . You want to insult me. You have no respect for the school and the prefects and monitors". At that time , Gautam did not answer him. Then , a thought came to his mind, revenge was due from the head boy and only hoped that his first name could save him.Vinod was in ninth standard and knew nothing more than his first name was Gautam and he studied class sixth division B.

All the classes were noisy in the break and the class sixth 'B' division was ahead in noise pollution. But minutes, after the bell rang and Ms Nilam Jadhav made an entry to make the class quiet. She was known to have good hold over the all classes in the school. A spectacled lady in her forties could be seen wearing blue, grey or black sarees who was expert in Marathi subject. After completing her own lectures in other classes, was assisgned a proxy one, she made up her mind to ask students finish their pending work and give rest to her brain. It was balancing act to keep the management satisfied and herself less stressed.

The main event unfolded when second standard boy asked for permission to enter the class. He said with improper atical English that Ms Flower wants to meet Gautam.He realized that the boy had come for him. So, he made up his mind to voluntarily stand up. Before could speak , Nilam miss asked Gautam Dubey to go with the messenger boy. Dubey was a naughty fellow, active only in troubling, breaking pencils , throwing or spoiling notebooks of other studious students. He was at his best in giving excuses for not completing his notes. Dubey's mother ensured that his notes were completed not by him but his elder sister, Ketki.She was overburdened to do two students job. Should parents exploit better sibling to ensure that the weaker ones are benefitted?

Dubey had no clue what was happening with him. Ms Nilam easily located him .He always sat on fourth bench in the row of nine benches. He sat in middle thinking that he would not get caught doing mischief . If noise comes, teacher in class normally had the tendency to check in last rows . But eight out of ten times , he was caught as he had enough notorious reputation.

Gautam was aware that messenger had come for him but Gautam Dubey was sent so it was an enjoying time for him.He was the director of confusion . It was created for fair purpose of saving himself .When you know what is the confusion and what is the solution, the feeling is similar to that of King. He was liking his moments of full control. Everything is in your control, you understand the situation what none does.

Gautam Dubey came after good fifteen minutes.He came back with smiling face who had went with long ,tense face and calculating the past events. The thought of severe punishment made him feel low when he was asked to meet teacher Flowers. He could not recollect any mischief for which he was not punished. But he had accepted to go with the boy younger than him after the teacher insisted on it. The teacher and the class also believed that Dubey junior would have done some thing wrong which had attracted the possible punishment. Once the bad name is printed on minds ,it becomes difficult to change into positive one.Can a child or adult image change in people's mind? How many good deeds are required to overcome a bad image?

When Dubey entered the punishment room on the first floor next to Principal's cabin along with lower ranked prefect of second standard. The ranking generally is decided in the standard the prefect is studying. Which also means number of years spent in school . The other simple meaning is seniority in school. He did not take permission as it was done for him by the messenger. He walked in two steps inside, when Vinod saw Dubey and said, "he is not the one we are looking for", then he turned to Miss and said whinning tone, "he was not there down in recess.Please call the real one ". Dubey needed time to understand and was confused in same manner as in the studies.His face achieved normalcy when Flower miss asked him to go back . Dubey came back with a naughty smile back on the face.He asked the off period teacher in indirect speech what Flower had said about sending the other Gautam. Both Dubey and the teacher set their eyes on Gautam Raut. . Raut was in between notorious and studious. The class along with teachers knew that he never failed in any exams but always commented while the teaching was teaching in class. He was taller than other Gautams and also better built with smart framed specs to hide his naughty side. He was a dependable player of the school cricket. He was unsure why he was called. After he was punished for talking in first Unit exams, he had kept himself away from acts where he would be blamed or could be complained against. Because of the incident during the exams, his father was called who warned him that if there was an complaint , his studies would be stopped. He would have to work in the family owned hotel. He was in state of fear of losing his studies. He reluctantly went to the first floor where head boy , head girl and all the prefects were waiting for the punishment to be given .

Ms Flower was sitting at the center of the table and as soon as Raut entered, she shouted , "Why did you splashed water on the head boy? You broke the discipline of the school".Even before Vinod could tell Miss that he was not the Gautam, he complained about. However,after hearing miss, the words of his father became louder in the both the halves of his brain.He hated the idea of serving other people and cleaning the food left-overs. He imagined how his life would be converted to a rag. In almost crying voice instantly , he said, " Miss , I did do not anything and I was in fifth class , C division in my sister's class. From tomorrow , I will not go anywhere . I will just remain in my class but please do not complaint to my parents".

Miss Flower realizing that she scolded the wrong boy ,had no option but to console him.She disliked her act but there are no rewind procedures. To accept mistakes in front of students without feeling bad is special.

When Raut returned to the class, the cry after effect could be seen on the face.Before Raut could enter the class, Gautam saw him from his place which was close to the door .Gautam got up to meet Miss Flower even before Raut uttering what happened.Raut seeing him, go to judgement room without any order from anyone created ideas that he was knowing everything .He made a failed attempt to ask the reality to him as Gautam had already gone.

Gautam realized the confusion had impacted Raut in a bad way and decided to end the confusion. Vinod had created the false situation to seek revenge but it was affecting a person who is not related. He went to the special room making himself strong enough to accept the act and the consequences . He told himself that he did not do it purposely, so it was okay to say,"I did it". He was playing with his friends and water splashed as he was running. He cannot be responsible as he was not the one who caused water to be accumulated there. So , the person responsible could be the gardener or the peon or sweeper who kept the job unfinished.He proved to himself that he is not at fault. He prepared for questions with answers ready. Every person should first prove innocence to themselves. The justification of self comes before others and it could win you any debate.

The door was open, Gautam stood at the entrance and asked for permission to enter with a voice lower than normal. Miss Flower saw him , not realizing about the complaint made against him and thought why he was called.Vinod in a high pitch said, "he is the boy who splashed water. He did the act purposely. He is culprit who broke the discipline. We must give him severe punishment". All this was said by Vinod pointing fingers towards Gautam. Miss Flower said in normal voice with affection , "Gautam , you go back to class", leaving Vinod and his supporters in state of a shock.

Gautam was such a student who never talked with his class mates during lectures. Apart from that he only spoke about studies. Gautam never stood first but the knowledge received went straight into safe deposit of his brain and it never evapourated. Never was his place changed by him without permission.No unwanted things and absolute no burden on the teacher.He listened and obeyed the teacher without any second thoughts. Miss Flower understood that what happened was just a normal child's play. He was her the most trusted student.One look towards Gautam was enough for her to realise what would have happened .It was like a mutual understanding transaction with no talk or receipt.When teacher gave the decision fully supporting him , he was extremely happy. Knowing the teacher trusted him so much and her accurate judgement about him gave the happiness which could be more than securing the highest marks in the school.

Gautam was shrewd in this particular incident. The water was splashed by mere accident . There was no motive to harm anyone. Most students know about other fellow not in their class by their face and at maximum theirs first names. Same was the case of Vinod about Gautam. He did not want to be punished for the act which was not done on purpose. He knew that confusion could be created by saying the first name only. There were other two Gautams .The children were at play without any negative incident. There was never a crime or offence hence Gautam wanted to avoid been caught. Miss Flower realized his feelings and even if the drama had not been taken place still the outcome would have been same as it was now. Good behavoiur , manners and honesty have more power to impress than any other thing. Many think that the such acts go unnoticed but people do observe it. Miss Flower had good judgement of students and also of handling of situations.She was clever enough to take proper decision. She did not justify to students why Gautam was spared. It would be too much of praise for him and there could be a possibility that he would take lightly such unwanted acts and deliberately commit such events. The probability was less but why to take any chance, thought Miss Flower.

HIDDEN SHAKESPEARE

In any school, the main function apart from giving knowledge through lectures of all walks in life, is to conduct exams. These assessments should be error free as much as possible. The deserving students should be able to prove themselves. Due the exams and the rules , the hidden Shakespeare was found.

The previous peon was leaking the questions in return of favor or money from students of class tenth. The semester one question papers were known to the students even before the exams. His bank accounts showed transactions of amount which was not within his reach to earn. The dates of the money credited was week before the exams on the day when the question paper was printed. The principal had taken the decision.

Bhimaji was latest addition to the staff of the school .He was appointed as a peon and in no time impressed everyone with his work . He was a man of twenty one years having a prominent nose with brown eyes and finely kept moustache. He was tall, medium built and his hair were always properly kept .His tenth passing was the highest level of education in his family.

The principal did not want any police interference to save the reputation of the school. There was no verbal disclosure of any kind . Kalyanji who was the old peon came to school after his service was discontinued . His acting of deying was upto the mark , making the teaching staff realise that all culprits having good acting skills. The principal could have disallowed him to enter the school premises but he wanted the see his face when the bank statement was shown. However excellent performer the bad person maybe , the proof brings such people to their knees. Same was the case with him.

Murthy sir was the head of the examination committee.The other members were Mrs Heena Ali and Ms Naina Kumar , work was distributed among the three without gender favouring of any kind. If the printing was question papers was given to Murthy sir of the Unit tests and the Semester was taken care by the ladies each doing one semester. The common factor was the office boy.

All the care was taken by Murthy and his team to keep wrong acts away during the examinations. All the pockets was checked and the bags were checked by Mr Kale himself.The lady security was also present to frisk the lady teachers. It gave the clear message about the seriousness involved. It also motivated all the staff to give priority to the exams and its secrecy.

Mr Subhash Kale, the principal wanted the office boy to not be familiar with English. According to him, the peon should know enough English which won't come in the way of fair conduction of exams. While printing and arranging, the office boy would come across the question papers and could easily remember the them and could pass on the corrupt parents or students.He trusted his teachers but his trust in office boys had become less. The leaking of question was very fresh in his mind. He also wanted to check if the person to be selected is lazy or casual.

So the principal decided to check his English knowledge and his work qualities. The interview was different from any other which could be cleared for not answering entirely.It was one of its kind where half knowledge was required to pass it. The reading session can also be faked by interviewees. The principal had to bring his wit gained over the years in conducting interview. The factor of keeping the school before him was motivating him. After thinking for about almost a day, he decided to give some reading practise sentences before conducting the interview. In the practise reading , he would give two simple two letter words at the start of first sentence of reading material.An employee from school would be there to help if required to pronounce two lettered words. If the interviewee did not even manage to read them in the interview, he would be faking it or not trying it or not having brains to relate .

Bhimaji was asked to be present in the school at 9.00 pm. He reached the school one and half hour before. He decided to make an impression by going early on the first day. He thought after his name and qualifications and experience , the interviewer would give him the job. Normally for the peon job , no private organisation bothers to have a reading or writing sessions. But he was surprised to receive a reading passage by the front desk clerk. She dutifully gave him the reading material and respectfully said," This is for your practise, in the interview , you will be asked to read another one.I can help if you need any ." she sounded very concerned and eager to help as she was ordered by the Principal.

He checked the printed paper which had six sentences. There was no heading and there was no connection of sentences with each other. He read it till the fifth one in less than six minutes. It was very simple task for him. He was tenth pass but served as office boy for three years at a reputed English speaking institute.

When he reached the third last word in last line, sudden thoughts of why is the reading interview for a person who would have nothing to do with it in the job. The mind kept finding answers about his work which will be just helping teachers in keeping files or documents. He could be asked to maintain discipline in the corridor or in office when parents or students were called. The principal would want him to keep his cabin clean, to serve him eatables or his favourite coffee. He said to himself that nowhere his reading ability was required. Even if the person wanting the peon post fails to comprehend all or a single word , he or anybody else should still get the job. In a private set up , the question of promotion will not make any sense , his mind gave a clear answer. He realised that objective of the interview was different and things are not what are seen by the naked eyes. He did not ask any anything to the cute and smiling saree clad front desk lady.

After waiting for a long time, Bhimaji was bored but he had to hide it. When the principal came , it brought smile on his face. He asked to go his cabin for the interview. Showing his face to take permission , the principal signaled him in . On entering , he saw the principal sitting on the chair with two empty chairs on either side and another one chair for the interviewee.It was well lit room but books rack of the right required dusting . The rectangular table was only had one sheet of paper which was the reading passage. He sat on the chair opposite to the interviewer when ordered . The principal was more interested in his education as he questioned " Did you go to school? What standard did you complete?". The interviewee answered respectfully that he was tenth pass from Satyavati Devi School in Mahad, Maharashtra.

Then the reading passage was handed by turning the page clockwise. The interview reading sentences were as follows

The organisation was on upward trend. Man and machine are important pillars to be managed for smooth work. They will make new policy on 29th May. The government should make education free for poor people. The schools should teach helping poor people as the most important duty.A king or ruler must keep the country happy. Knowledge is dangerous tool in hands of negative person.

Bhimaji read all the two and three lettered words and purposely not reading others words. He left alone or read half , the longer words. The result was his reading was not making any sense . But his trick worked and the principal was gave out expressions confirming the office boy job. This balanced approach saved him and he got the job. It matched the expectations of the interviewer perfectly. The correct pronunciation created doubts but Bhimaji got the benefit of the doubt and the job.

He had to fool others in school about his ability to read and understand English language. The secret of knowing more had to be kept till he worked in that organisation. So the main work to survive was faking along with other official duties. He hoped that the' extra-critical work' does not over burden him.

Murthy was told about the unavailability of Ms Ali and he was given the task to complete the pending work and in front of other teachers. Now he had to do the   Ms Ali's job to print the question papers. He disliked sudden work because always planned the day for smooth transition into night sleep. There no show of displeasure on his face which is possible for only experienced employees. There were negative talks about female way of working by teachers having male egos. Murthy overheard such conversations which made him more determined to finish the work effectively . He did not classify problems on basis of gender. According to him ,problems are general and family members must overcome problems together.

He made a mental plan of the chapters to be finished and also to accommodate the extra work . Satisfied , he began with the newly assigned work by calling Bhimaji to the printing room. He taught him how to do the printing and the peon learnt but the speed of printing was slow. Nevertheless the work was on .

His lectures were swapped with Ms Yadhav and Mr Bhushan in the studious fifth B and balanced sixth D so that Murthy could focus on printing . But at the eleventh hour, the Principal had to take them for urgent meeting called by the trustees regarding an Industrial Visit of the school to a private sector bank. It also included advertisement of the school. The bank was scoring on Social Cause points and creating a name for itself . So arrangements had to be made keeping security and control over the event as it was first such bank had approached the school . The trustees were eyeing the marketing and promotion of the school and more admissions for the next academic year.

The principal and other four teachers were required to be the part of the adverstisement and promotion. This meant that the he was required him to be present in the class and the exam work would be delayed . He had to wait after working hours of the school. The work would be without over time pay but it did not affect his interest in the exam duty. Out of seven subjects ,only English question needed changes. The English teacher was the person who had studied Master's degree from Oxford University under a rule by U.K. King. The persons selected from India and other parts of world could chance through an NGO to complete the post graduation degree. He or she would learn the language at an afforadable fee paid by the NGO. After completing the degree, it was mandatory for the person to serve as the subject teacher in financially weaker school directed by the NGO in countries which they belonged.

Among the eight selected one was Mr Devendra Bedi, the new English teacher of the school. After going to England was cut short to Dev Bedi. A tall man in his late twenties, clean shaven and compeletely bald. On the knowledge front , the students of the school were lucky as he was a passionate teacher. Only problem was that of U.K. accent as it was not neutralised to an extent that students were able to understand. The written notes and question papers were most of words which were unfamiliar and tough for students . The other teachers had trouble trying to hide their little knowledge of such words. At times, students ask the teachers about the unknown words used in the English lectures by Dev sir . It was just to test them. The teachers said that they will say it tomorrow or they will find it and help them. The talks to change his accent to a neutral one were becoming louder and would reach the ears of management sooner or later.

The question paper needs to be balanced , not too difficult neither so simple that students do not value the subject , teacher and the knowledge. The best student needs to earn the highest mark and the below average student should be able to manage the passing marks. This was the followed by the school as per the guidelines given by the principal. So when the paper was set by him or any teacher , it needed to be restructured by the Exam Committee . The reconstruction required perfect knowledge of English vocabulary . Any change in the question paper should be such without making it weird. Unthoughtful changing of words or sentences may lead to an incomprehensible abstract for the students. The Examination Committee required to be careful of such things and it strongly felt that vocalbulary concern needed resolve from the management.

Murthy left the Anglo -English paper as he called it, in the printing room and went to conduct the lecture on a short notice. Bhimaji informed him that all other subjects question papers were ready. All others subject question papers were ready for printing only English paper was disturbing him but he had to concentrate on the lecture. A successful teacher has to be present in present tense and not in past or future. His mind tried to focus on the solutions making him realised that Bhimaji and one more person was there to help him. The negative part of brain made it clear that there were little hopes from the clerk cum cashier cum admim executive, Suryakant Chouhan. He was man in his early thirties ,a medium height and built with an agreeable face. He had affinity of yellow colour so always wore trouser of shade of that colour. Many doubted he wore same trouser everyday. Before leaving the printing room he said a louder tone closing the door, "Bhimaji…. Could you? ..a…. if you can get simpler words ….. and make the question paper better." The message was for Mr Suryakant through Bhimaji.

The little hopes were having the equation in Murthy 's mind. The hopes from Bhimaji were same as expected from failure student to complete an intelligent task and the expectations from Suryakant were that from just passing student. Suryakant was man made because of his brother who was political friend of the trustee. He started calculating , he wished that any one of them or both become Shakespeare and get the simple synonyms for the words in the question paper. He wanted it to happen at any how. They had an hour and fifty minutes to work like the great dramatist and save him from sitting late in office. Maybe more late because mental fatigue during lectures could take more time. After completing the once cancelled lectures, he went to the printing room. Not bothering to wash face and drink the lukewarm water which he did on any other day.

Trying to hear the voices or any noise, he opened the door to find none of them inside. He then checked the work and found that Shakespeare had done the work. No extra hours of waiting after the toiling day! Bhimaji entered the room when Murthy was sitting on the chair in front of the computer with his brain full of happy feeling. The peon said, " Sir, the work has been done so we don't have to wait . " Murthy already knew it that they will be leaving office on time as all the tasks were completed. Still, he smiled at Bhimaji not wanting to take the credit of giving of the job done news.He smiled same as the smile on hearing the joke on second time. Happily , he collected the question paper set and submitted in the office. When a hard working person finds good help from his juniors or colleagues , the motivation and satisfaction reaches a new high . Here the expectations was less so the satisfaction was on the higher side.

After the exams were conducted smoothly , the principal appreciated   the entire Exam Committee for the good show. Ms Ali came to Murthy sir in the break and said, " Thankyou sir because of you I could take leave and be with my son. Also you managed everything without any problems.Now ,the staff can say that we don't require me... " with a smile on her face. He replied with a laughter, " Madam, it is team effort.....".Having said that he realized that Shakespeare played an important role in it. But he didn't know who was his Shakespeare.

He wanted to know who between the two did the work like Shakespeare. According to him, the whole school should be thankful for the brilliant work done. He was getting credit of someone's else. The person got the correct synonyms and made the question paper as per the requirements.Even the sentences became better. His thoughts told him that there were too many corrections to be done by luck or by mistake . Along with checking answer sheets, he had to find answer of the two questions regarding who and how it was possible.

The question papers should be made in accordance of the standard and as per instructions of the Education Department. Mr Dev level was higher than the required standards but in such cases the teachers should come down . A true teacher is a one who understand the level of students and can himself or herself mould accordingly. All levels of learning and knowledge must be known to teachers. He would need time to transform into a better version of teacher. The earlier , the better for everyone.

Murthy wanted to thank his Shakespeare. Bhimaji was the Shakespeare who helped Murthy in making the question paper suitable for the standard seventh. He never wanted him to know the truth. He thought why he did it in the first place , inviting the trouble. It could cost him his job in the school. He decided to find ways to keep Murthy from himself. He was not any authority or any high post to give orders to any teacher like Murthy to stop the search. He had to be alert and equally smart to avoid the Murthy to find the reality. A thought that he was negative started to make place in his mind but the answer was that he was saving himself from knowledge problem.

Suryakant always wanted to take credit of work and tasks done by others as he had never done any job successfully himself. He never bothered to make himself better as he got everything in hands easily. He always told everyone how difficult it was for him to get the post in the college. The truth was never hidden about the contacts that helped in his employment. Unless you try things on your own, none can get knowledge. Going into the core of the matter will result in achieving a sound level of understanding.

There was one such incident about his credit seeking , When the Hindi teacher cheque book which went missing for five days. The book was by mistake kept by the teacher in the next locker which belonged to Mohit Shah who was doing internship with school since last four months. He was the man who kept himself away from female colleagues. He spoke to the other females in the school only about work nothing more or nothing less. The staff wondered and gossiped about the reason of his strange behaviour. When Mohit found the bank book in his locker. He did not think anything other than to hand over the lost bank document to Suryakant who take care of 'lost and found'.

Suryakant was busy showing he was loaded with at his work station as always. Most of the work was handled by the teachers. There was not a single file or document on the table but on seeing Mohit, he manged to get some files. He said to Suryakant patiently that found Yadav teacher's cheque book and requested him to give it to her. Suryakant replied looking the file said," You give to Yadav madam, she would be searching for it. Your internship ends today so give it without fail. I heard that after your internship are going to your village for the next seven days", trying to say in suggestive tone. He was aware that Mohit avoided any dealings with females.He managed to control the his ninety five percentage of his smile while suggesting but the rest was seen on his face. As expected Mohit gave the cheque book to Suryakant and in requesting tone, " you understand the importance of the bank documents, please give to Yadav madam".

Suryakant understood that it was a chance to prove that he was good in helping and finding things for people. He had the bank book, he can so easily show that he worked to find it and help the teacher and the school. After confirming that his locker was clean enough to be checked by anyone, he asked the peons to take his keys and search lockers of the staff. The third day , most of his day in office was spent in fake finding the thing which he already had . On the fourth day , he handed the bank book to Yadav maam saying , "You were desperately searching for this book, I got it for you. I found it in the papers lying on the table near your locker. None searched there but my instincts made me realised that it would be somewhere near the locker. I took time to find apart from my normal work. If my inner feelings would have hinted earlier, I would have been given it to you earlier", he said with self pride.

She replied in a satisfying tone ," Thankyou, all helped me to search the cheque book but are the one who got it. Your instincts are special."All the teachers including Yadav maam were happy but his over effort created suspicion in their minds. Whatever it may be , she was happy to get the cheque leaves book before complaining and give details to bank how it was missing.

After three days, Mohit came to the staff room and gave the missing page of cheque booklet which was request page to get new book. Yadav maam wanted to get new one as there were few pages remaining. She had kept the request page differently to submit in bank. It was below the book. He failed to see the separate page and gave the book to Suryakant . The request page was left in his bag. After realizing it, he came to school to help the owner. He told the entire story leaving the woman understand that Suryakant took the credit of searching the missing book. He wanted to show the school that the was capable of doing a task which others cannot do. She went to the principal after checking time table. She had around forty five minutes before her next lecture. She entered in his cabin taking permission in a tone which made Mr Subhash realised something was not right. He permitted her and offered a chair to sit. He also tried to balance the situation by asking her politely " Yadav teacher, how is everything? Her tone was bit higher and he could feel frustration in it. She said , "Sir , Suryakant had the cheque book with him from the day it was given to him by Mohit . He did acting of finding the booklet. He wasted the time of entire school asking the staff members to search the bank document. It is very bad on the part of an employee playing games with the school. He did not think about my state of mind in those days. I demand a strict action against him." The principal was aware that she was rightfully complaining about Suryakant. He said to the Hindi teacher in an assuring tone , "I will have a word with him and see that he or none from our school including me will get involved in such acts. Credit seeking for work not done or to show how better an employee is than others by manipulation is unacceptable."

He knew Suryakant even before he joined school. He was selected by interview which was based on friendship where educational qualifications did not matter . When any person is employed with the above ' Friendship' then the employer looses the right to question him or her anything in future.Mr Subhash knew that to expect   a changed behaviour from Suryakant was useless. But he decided to talk about the matter with Suryakant so that it would atleast make him think his foul plays are not unnoticed.

The principal had to attend the special training education camp in the remote village of Marathawada . These camps were started by the UK and India in an agreement to help financially weaker families. It wanted to change the lives of less fortunate students. In his absence, Murthy sir was given the resposibility of handling the school affairs for the next fifteen days. It was an opportunity to find out his Indian Shakespeare. It was confirmed when he understood that the English teacher will be going to Delhi to get his passport work done. The passport documents verification had some complications which would take atleast five days. It is easier to convert such opportunities into reality when we have final authority in an organisation.

He called Suryakant from office to the vacant cabin just next to the principal cabin. He highly respected the principal and so did not to use his chair. He asked Bhimaji to call him and the other peon was sent to the ground floor to help the watchmen to manage the parents of pre-primary students. The other peon had the habit of listening to crucial matters and passing it to others and even creating rumours.

Suryakant entered the cabin with less formal permission by waiting at the entrance before he was asked to come in.He requested the follower, Bhimaji to get butter milk which he brought in his bag. Murthy sir was sitting in the cabin which had not A.C. and unoiled fan making noise. Suryakant sat in the chair opposite to Murthy which was selected after checking that the four legs were of equal length. Bhimaji entered with only two glasses of butter milk , then Murthy insisted, "I told you, get one for yourself and also get stool as the other chair is not proper." The science teacher and now the stand in principal was giving value to peon which was visible to both.

After the office boy was seated, Murthy said with false praise and alert enough not making anybody realise it, " Suryakant without you the English question paper was not possible", in an appreciating tone. The sentence took the credit seeker on the highest gear and the original speaker had to stop. Suryakant started to praise himself with tone of exaggeration.He said, "Only I could do it. It was not at all a task which could be manged by experts. I have improved my …. words number by constant …. hardly working ."Murthy corrected by saying " you mean   to say vocabulary ….. and you worked for it." He did not want to rectify further. The message was clear and loud about his level of English. It indicated strongly that Bhimaji is the desi Shakespaere.Murthy knew that he will not say it directly but he wanted to hear it from his mouth even after all the understanding of what would have happened. Bhimaji was happy that his job was not in trouble after hearing the praise of Suryakant.

Murthy drank the buttermilk making sound to others to show how delicious it was. He then revealed the reason of the ordering the three glasses. Trying to sound real, he said, " Today , I got the message that our school has been included in the poem writing competition. So, I decided to have butter milk instead of tea. When our school will become victorious , we also celebrate in presence of the Principal. We got included late in it. We got the information just one hour back. Our English teacher is gone out. As said earlier, Suryakant you are the best in English so the responsibility goes on your shoulders. Time is running out for us and our school. We have to submit it today or else the school will get a bad name." Hearing it ,Suryakant felt irritated which could be seen in his movements. After the Murthy sir completed his words, he realised that he was at unwanted place. What he could do was to only nod, showing acceptance to all what Murthy sir said.

Murthy pointed at his glass signalling Bhimaji to pick them all.While he was collecting the empty glasses, Murthy with authority and loud enough to make an impact on the second listener, said , "Complete the poem , it should not be less than ten lines . You can have any rhyming scheme.At end of the day , keep that completed paper in the blue folder . If not ,you might loose your post in the school. That's the message from the Management as the competition will decided whether the school gets the advertisement , recognitions and funds." He had to manage to say the last four sentences before the peon leaves the temporary cabin. Suryakant, the first listener felt that it would have been better if he had no ears on that day.

Murthy after seeing Bhimaji was out of the room, he said firmly ,"Ensure that you finish the prestigious task and keep in the brown folder." The pace was slower than the before and the color brown was said with marked stress. He thought that Suryakant would enquire about the change from blue to brown. Since there was no such asking ,Murthy had to say ," I repeat, brown folder," using acting skills to a good effect.

Suryakant tried many times to call the principal but there was no response. He was surprised not understanding the reason behind it. Murthy was smart enough to convince the principal for it . It was easy for him to use the recent bad episode of the cheque book. The administration in charge had to believe that his job was in under threat because his calls were got converted to missed calls. There was no point in taking help as his uncle, the political friend of principal might find him in fault and he would have to face anger, his brain decided him.

Finally , the time was nearing when the Shakespaere will not be hidden. All the things hinted that now he would have the proof of his belief.It was normal day for other teachers, Suryakant did not disclose anything to anyone . None would trust him especially after the bank booklet false credit seeking, maybe he himself had sensed it so the things were under wraps. Bhimaji being latest one in the staff still had to be close to share the information with others in the organisation.

Murthy kept himself free of lectures by balancing the lectures among the other teachers. He also had the responsibility of managing the school. In the second last lecture , he arranged the folders of both the colours. The blue one on the left hand side of the table and the brown on the right. He wanted to witness the entire event but his mind denied it. He did want not any mistake to happen. Since he had no work , he was becoming more and more restless. He controlled himself and tried to calm himself down. Finally, he went to the canteen and sipped his favourite black coffee to keep everything normal. His mind confirmed that everything was going to in its proper place and if it was not the case then there could be other way of catching his Shakespeare.

Out of the two, first was Suryakant as his job was in danger . It was written on his face that there was no other to save his job other than getting the poetry on paper. He went to new cabin straight . He entered it and saw two folders which was not told to him. He decided to keep the poetry in the other folder and see the fun when it would not be found by Murthy sir. Then, he would help by finding the paper kept purposely in the wrong coloured folder. And take the credit of finding the paper as per his known behaviour. But the picture of him walking on road to get job was played by his brain if things went wrong. So, he kept the poem in the right folder.

In the cabin, fifteen before the ring of the last lecture , Bhimaji carrying the poetry entered the smaller cabin. He ensured none was around . He, like most lower rank employees knew the place from the staircase to check if any person is in the corridor . His brain was working that he being the Shakespeare was trying to save the job of Suryakant. Infact he was saving his own job did not struck him.He checked the cabin was not locked just by pushing lightly by hand and finding it not occupied by anyone and entered in. Wasting no time , found the blue folder, in one action folded the paper and kept it neatly in the blue folder. He left the cabin closing it with same soft feet as the time of entering. He went to ring the much awaited bell of last lecture. There were more than seven minutes for the bell, he was quicker than his calculation and he felt better about that.

The bell rang asking Murthy sir to come to his cabin from the school canteen. He reached the cabin calmly using the stairs.Finding none of the two , he went to the table and was happy to find the folders not empty. With smile, he removed the poetry from both the folders as things were falling as per plan. The smiled broaden more when he read the papers in the brown folder . He knew the poem was a copy from the magazine published two years back of their school. But it was of nine lines only. It was no surprise as Suryakant always showed his low capabililty.The blue folder had Suryakant's poem was one of better poem ever heard of eleven lines. Shakespeare is not hidden and now he had the proof of it. Both Suryakant and Bhimaji acted as expected.

He called Bhimaji and said enthusiastically," you are an expert in English". Bhimaji replied reluctantly," Wha….What, you have to say Murthy sir ", the peon's face showed fear. Seeing straight in the eyes of Bhimaji, Murthy sir said assuringly , "The secret of yours knowing will not reach anybody." Hearing the last sentence , the office boy felt relaxed as sensed by the acting p rincipal. He told Murthy sir how his working at the institute polished his English . Murthy sir said further with smile, " From today, I will call you Shakespeare".

None can forget their school days whatever age and status is attained. In this book, there hilarious incidents of which will take everybody down the memory lane to their schools. You will find characters similar to your friends , the teachers, peons and atmosphere during those days. There incidents of hitting others.... trying to escape punishment... using same names advantage... teachers, staff and peons issues.

www.ingramcontent.com/pod-product-compliance
Lightning Source LLC
LaVergne TN
LVHW092031190726
843493LV00002B/646